HONEY PIE PONY'S BOOK

A Fun with Fillies Adventure

by Victoria Muschinske

Scholastic Inc.

New York   Toronto   London   Auckland   Sydney   Mexico City   New Delhi   Hong Kong   Buenos Aires

ISBN 0-439-70471-5

Designer: Emily Muschinske
Illustrations: Lisa and Terry Workman
Photographs: Emily Muschinske

12 11 10 9 8 7 6 5 4 3 2 1   5 6 7 8 9 10/0

Printed in the U.S.A.
First Scholastic printing, May 2005

TABLE OF CONTENTS

Get Ready for a FUN with FILLIES Adventure!

Hi, my berry sweet friend! It's me, Strawberry Shortcake, and my pretty pony pal, Honey Pie.

Join us as we meet Honey Pie's pony pals, create fun crafts, make yummy treats, and play great games together! If you're ready, grab your Filly Craft Kit and let's get started!

Welcome to Ice Cream Island, where I live near my pony friends. My home is called Honey Pony Pastures.

3

Honey Pie Pony and Strawberry Shortcake's Tips for Getting Started

1. **Set up your berry own play space to create your pony projects! Cover your area with newspaper to keep everything clean and neat.**

2. **Ask an adult to help you collect everything you need before you start a craft or yummy recipe.**

3. **Whenever you see this picture throughout the book, it means that you can find what you need in your Filly Craft Kit.**

4. **Some of the materials you'll need can be found around your house. You can get other materials at a grocery or at a craft store.**

5. **Whenever you see this picture throughout the book, you'll know to ask for a grown-up's help.**

Berry Funny

Q: What is the hardest thing about learning to ride a horse?

A: The ground!

Getting Ready to Use the Kitchen

1. **Before getting started, put on an apron and pull back your hair so that it doesn't get in your way—or in your food!**

2. **Wash your hands with soap and warm water.**

3. **Once you've chosen a recipe, get all of the ingredients and utensils together. Then follow each step closely.**

4. **Clean up as you cook. Remember to put the ingredients away as you use them.**

5. **Always ask a grown-up for help when you use utensils in the kitchen.**

Berry Funny

Q: What's black and white and eats like a horse?

A: A zebra!

Who are the Strawberryland Fillies?

Honey Pie Pony is Strawberry Shortcake's special friend. She's traveled all over, but her favorite place is Ice Cream Island.

Blueberry Sundae is Blueberry Muffin's pretty pony pal.

Milkshake is Angel Cake's fast filly friend.

Orange Twist is Orange Blossom's pretty pony.

Ginger Snap's sweet filly friend is Cookie Dough.

Turn the page to see how you can decorate your hair to look as pretty as Honey Pie Pony's mane and tail!

Pretty Pony Hair Clips

Honey Pie Pony always wears pretty decorations in her mane and on her tail. You can design barrettes for your hair too!

What You Need

- Barrettes
- Foam pieces
- Double-sided tape tabs
- Jewels

2. Stick the sticky tab to the wide end of a hair clip. Peel off the top layer of the double-stick tab.

1. Peel off one side of a double-stick tab. Ask a grown-up for help, if you need it.

3. Press a green foam leaf to the double-stick tab.

4. **Use another sticky tab to tape a yellow flower on top of the leaf.**

5. **With another tab, attach a pretty jewel to the center of the flower. Clip the barrette into your hair. How pretty!**

Here's More:

How many hair clip styles can you make?

🍓 Use the blue circle shapes to make a hair clip that you or Blueberry Sundae, Blueberry Muffin's pretty filly friend, could wear.

🍓 Use the bows to make a Cookie Dough ribbon hair clip for yourself or for Ginger Snap's sweet filly friend.

🍓 Make a flower hair clip with four green leaves. Do you think Orange Twist, Orange Blossom's fun filly friend, will like it?

Turn the page to see Honey Pie Pony and her pony friends at play!

Ponies at Play

Honey Pie Pony and all her pony friends come to life in Honey Pony Pastures!

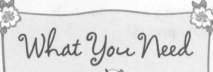

What You Need

- 5 ponies and stands
- Strawberry Shortcake and stand
- 6 pony fences and stands
- Strawberry Shortcake cling stickers

2. Each pony has two small slits on the bottom of its feet. Take one of the ponies and slide a stand into each of the small slits. Now the pony can stand!

1. Arrange the five ponies in front of you on a table or on the floor, along with the stands.

3. Repeat step 2, adding stands for all five ponies. Add Strawberry Shortcake's stands too, so she can join Honey Pie and the other ponies.

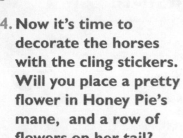

4. **Now it's time to decorate the horses with the cling stickers. Will you place a pretty flower in Honey Pie's mane, and a row of flowers on her tail?**

5. **Will you decorate Blueberry Muffin's pony, Blueberry Sundae, in blueberries? Will you give bows to Ginger Snap's pony, Cookie Dough? You decide!**

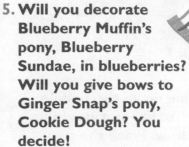

6. **Take your six candy-cane-striped fences and add stands to each one. Set up the fences to create the field where the ponies romp and run.**

7. **Now give Strawberry Shortcake a basket filled with strawberries! Will you add an extra pink and green bow to her hat?**

Here's More: Peel off the cling stickers and decorate your ponies a different way each time you play!

Turn the page to make a pasture for the ponies!

Ponies in the Pasture

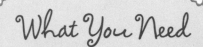
Give your ponies a place to play!

What You Need

- Scissors
- Pencil
- Mug
- Lid from a juice bottle
- Tape
- Construction paper
  (2 sheets of yellow,
  and 1 sheet each of
  orange, red, blue, green,
  brown, and white)
- 5 ponies and stands

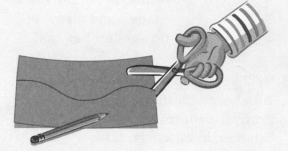

2. Draw a curvy line down the middle of a green sheet of paper. Cut along the curve you drew. Place the two curved shapes next to each other on the yellow paper so they look like grassy hills.

1. Lay two sheets of yellow paper flat. Tape them together, as shown.

3. Trace the bottom of a mug onto orange paper. Cut out the round shape. This will be the sun.

4. Trace the juice lid onto the blue paper in three or four overlapping circles. Cut out the wavy shape for a cloud. Add a second cloud to your sky.

7. Draw a tall rectangle with a rounded top onto red paper. Cut out the shape and place it next to the barn. This is the silo.

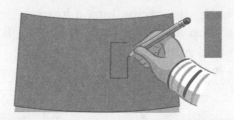

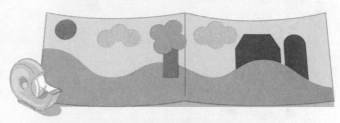

5. Draw a rectangle onto brown paper to make a tree trunk. Then, using the juice lid, trace overlapping circles onto green paper. Cut the shapes out to make leaves. Now you have a tree.

8. Tape all your shapes to the yellow paper. Now bring out your ponies, fences, and cling stickers. Place them in front of the pasture. Have fun in the sun, Honey Pie Pony and friends!

6. Draw a rectangle onto red paper and add a triangle on top. Cut out the shape. Now cut off the top of the triangle. This is the barn.

Turn the page to see how you can make yourself sparkle!

Lovely Locket Necklace

Just like the ponies like lots of pretty colors, you can make yourself a colorful, sparkly, jeweled locket.

What You Need

- Film canister or small vitamin bottle
- Jewels
- Glitter
- Colored tissue paper
- 30 inches of yarn, string, or ribbon
- Craft glue
- Scissors

2. **Tie the ends of a string into a knot. Push the loop end of the string through the hole and pull it through. The knot will stop it.**

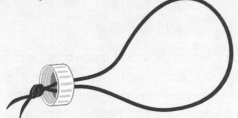

1. **Remove the cap from the top of the film canister or small bottle. Ask an adult to poke a hole through it.**

3. **Spread glue onto the top of the cap and stick a small piece of tissue paper to it. It's okay if it wrinkles.**

4. Spread glue on the outside of the film canister or bottle. Cover it with tissue paper, too.

5. After the glue dries, spread more glue over the tissue paper on the outside of the film canister or bottle.

6. Roll the canister or bottle in glitter and set it aside to dry.

7. Glue jewels to the cap of the canister. Let dry.

8. When everything is dry, brush the loose glitter off of your new locket and hang it around your neck.

Here's More: What special keepsake will you place inside your lovely locket?

Turn the page for lots of fun and games!

Honey Doodle's Bee Toss Game

$\mathcal{D}$id you know that Honey Doodle is Honey Pie Pony's pal? The two love to play together. With this game, you can have fun, too!

First you make the game, and then you play it!

What You Need

- Scissors
- Craft glue
- Foam or cardboard egg carton
- 4 sheets of colored construction paper in green, yellow, red, and orange
- Black marker
- 24-inch string

1. Cut the top off of an egg carton. Then, cut two long strips out of the carton's top. These will be the handle—and the flower's stem!

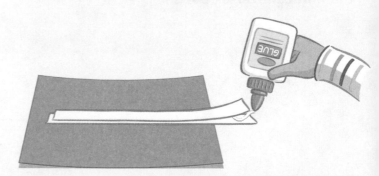

2. Glue the two strips together. Then, wrap a piece of green construction paper around the strips and glue in place. Let dry.

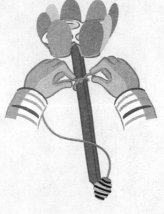

3. Cut a group of four egg cups off of the egg carton. This is your flower.

4. Next, it's time to make the flower petals. Draw a U-shape onto a piece of colored paper. Cut it out. You will need eight U-shapes. Make them different colors, if you like. Glue the petals to the sides of the egg-cup flower.

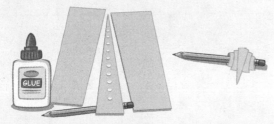

5. To make the bee, first cut a long triangle of yellow paper. Put glue dots along one side, almost to the bottom, as shown. Wrap the paper around a pencil. Let dry for about 15 minutes. Remove the pencil.

6. Use the black marker to draw stripes on your bee. Then glue the bee to one end of the string. Tie the other end of the string to the green flower stem.

Here's How to Play:

Hold the stem of the flower. Toss the bee into the air with a forward swing of your arm. Try to catch the bee in the egg cups. See how many times in a row you can catch the bee!

Turn the page for another pony game that you can make and play!

Honey Pie Pony's Horseshoe Game

See how good you are at tossing and throwing when you play this game!

1. Lay the cardboard flat. Cut 1-inch slits around the bottom of the toilet paper tube. Flatten the slits and glue the tube into the middle of the base.

2. Put glue all over the cardboard base and on the tube. Wrap the base and tube in colored tissue paper to decorate it.

What You Need

- A 9-x-12-inch piece of cardboard (you can recycle a cereal box by flattening it)
- Colored tissue paper
- Construction paper
- Manila folder
- 10 pennies
- Masking tape
- Toilet paper tube
- Scissors
- Craft glue

3. Cut a piece of construction paper to cover the top hole in the tube and glue it on. Decorate the base with fun shapes such as stars, flowers, and grass.

5. Tape the pennies to one of the horseshoes to give it weight, and lay the other horseshoe on top. Wrap tape around the horseshoe to hold the two sides together. Cover with colored tissue paper.

4. Keep the manila folder folded. Draw a horseshoe on the folder and cut it out. Unfold the folder and you will have two horseshoes. The horseshoes should be about the size of an adult's hand.

6. Now you're done and ready to play!

Turn the page to see how to play the horseshoe game!

How to Play Honey Pie Pony's Horseshoe Game

Horse around with your berry best friends to see who is good at playing your new horseshoe game!

1. Place the horseshoe base on the floor. Take two big steps away from it.

3. Toss the horseshoe at the peg you made from the cardboard roll. Try to loop the horseshoe around the peg.

2. Hold your horseshoe by the round end. Point the horseshoe ends at your game board.

2 points

1 point

4. You get a point if the horseshoe lands touching the board. You get two points if you hook the horseshoe around the peg.

Honey Pie Pony's Oatmeal Fun Dough

What fun shapes do you like to make?

2. **Now it's time to form the play dough into shapes. Use your fingers and a plastic knife to sculpt a star with five points.**

3. **Add a tail to the star to make it a shooting star!**

What You Need

- 1 cup flour
- 2 cups dry oatmeal
- 1 part water
- Utensils: Bowl, plastic knife, measuring cups, plastic wrap

Here's More: See if you can make a pony or a cat out of the dough! Hint: Use toothpicks to hold the shapes of the animals together. To smooth the surface of your shapes, wet your fingers first.

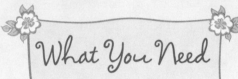

1. **Mix the flour, oatmeal, and water together in a bowl. Wrap the dough in plastic wrap and let it sit for an hour.**

Turn the page to help Honey Pie find her way to Strawberryland!

Filly Fun and Games

Honey Pie Pony's Spelling Bee Puzzle

Help Honey Pie Pony find Strawberry Shortcake. Honey Pie can only step on the spaces with the letters that spell STRAWBERRYLAND.

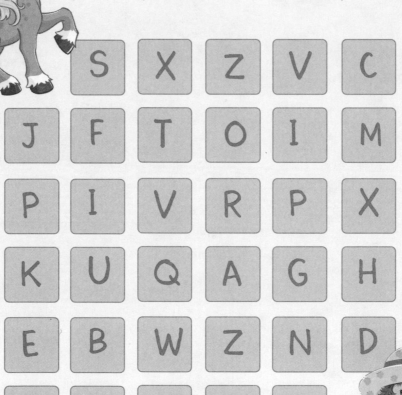

S	X	Z	V	C
J	F	T	O	I	M
P	I	V	R	P	X
K	U	Q	A	G	H
E	B	W	Z	N	D
R	R	Y	L	A

Turn to page 38 for the answers.

Honey Pie's Horse Sense

*C*an you match the names of the different parts of
Honey Pie Pony's body to each of those sections in the picture?

1. **Honey Pie Pony's mane**

2. **Honey Pie Pony's tail**

3. **Honey Pie Pony's hooves**

4. **Honey Pie Pony's back**

5. **Honey Pie Pony's forelock**

Hint: Forelock is a lock of hair
that falls on a horse's forehead.

Turn to page 38 for the answers.

Turn the page to see if you can spot
all the differences in Pony Pastures!

21

Honey Pie Pony and Friends Match-Up Game
Can you find what's different between the two pictures?

Turn to page 38 for the ten answers.

22

Turn the page to make some berry tasty honey treats!

Honey-licious Honey Bars

Do you like honey? Honey Pie Pony likes honey too!

What You Need

- 1/2 cup softened butter
- 1/2 cup brown sugar, packed
- 3 tablespoons honey
- 1/4 cup white sugar
- 1/2 teaspoon vanilla
- 1 egg
- 1 cup flour
- 1/2 teaspoon baking powder
- 1/4 teaspoon salt
- 1 1/2 cups oats
- 2 cups crispy rice cereal (such as Rice Krispies®)
- Utensils: Measuring cups and spoons, 2 mixing bowls, wooden spoon, greased 9-x-9-inch pan

Makes: 9 squares

1. Have an adult preheat the oven to 350°F. In a mixing bowl, cream together the egg, honey, two sugars, vanilla, and butter.

2. In another bowl, combine the flour, baking powder, salt, and oats.

3. Combine the two mixtures together. Stir.

6. Bake for 30 minutes until brown. When done, have an adult take the pan out of the oven.

4. Fold the rice cereal into the mixture, using a wooden spoon.

7. Cool for half an hour. Cut into squares. The bars will become crispy and crunchy, just like Honey Pie likes them!

5. The dough will be stiff. Press into a greased 9-x-9-inch pan.

Turn the page to make Honey Doodle's favorite snack!

Honey Doodle's Honey Jacks

This treat is sweet, crunchy, and fun to munch!

What You Need

- Ready-made popcorn
- 1/2 stick butter or margarine
- 1/2 cup honey
- Utensils: 9-x-12-inch baking dish, small saucepan, serving bowl, wooden spoon

Makes: 4 servings

1. Ask an adult to preheat the oven to 375°F. Place the popcorn in a baking dish.

2. Melt the butter in a small saucepan over low heat. Add honey. Stir until golden.

3. Use a spoon to drizzle the butter and honey mixture onto the popcorn.

4. Bake uncovered for 10 minutes. Have an adult remove the dish from the oven. Let cool for 15 minutes so that the Honey Jacks get crunchy.

Berry Funny

Q: Where do you take sick ponies?

A: To the horsepital!

Turn the page to make a berry refreshing drink!

Sparkling Honey-ade

Here's a fizzy, fun drink
for you to enjoy!

What You Need

- 1 cup honey
- 1 cup water
- 1.5 liters of seltzer
- ½ can (4 ounces) of lemonade concentrate
- Ice
- Lemon slice
- Utensils: 2-quart pitcher, knife, saucepan, long wooden spoon, juice glasses

Makes: 8 servings or glasses (one pitcher)

1. With a grown-up's help, heat the water in a saucepan until hot. The water does not need to boil.

2. Dissolve the honey completely in the hot water. Stir frequently.

3. **Add the lemonade concentrate to the mixture. Stir until the concentrate dissolves completely. Remove from the heat. Let cool.**

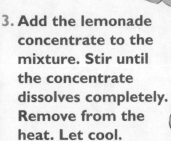

4. **Open the seltzer bottle over the sink. First, untwist the top a little to let the gas escape. Count to ten. Then open the bottle completely. Pour the seltzer into the pitcher.**

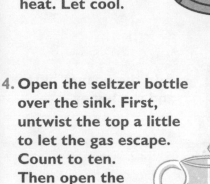

5. **Add the "syrup" mixture to the seltzer. Stir. But don't stir too much or you will stir the fizz out!**

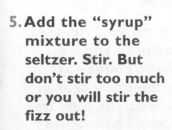

6. **Fill each glass with ice. Pour your honey-ade over the ice.**

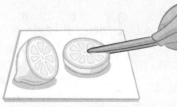

7. **Garnish with a lemon slice. To cut the lemon slice, have an adult lay the lemon on its side and cut it down the middle. Then cut it from the center to the edge. The slit will help it sit on the edge of the glass.**

Turn the page to make a milkshake with Milkshake!

Milkshake's Milkshake

Angel Cake's pony pal, Milkshake, loves milkshakes. Do you, too?

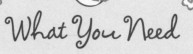

What You Need

- 3 tablespoons peanut butter
- 2 cups milk
- 2 cups ice cubes
- 7 ounces of frozen vanilla yogurt
- 4 tablespoons honey
- Utensils: Blender, ice cream scoop, measuring spoons and cups, glass

2. Add the peanut butter and the honey.

3. Scoop up and add in the frozen yogurt. Then add the milk.

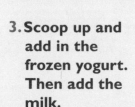

1. Pour the ice into the blender.

4. Blend for 2 minutes, or until the ice cube chunks are completely broken apart. The mixture should be smooth and frothy.

On the Trail Trail Mix

Take a tasty treat with you on a hike, or while on a visit to a pony farm.

What You Need

- 2 cups pretzels
- ½ cup raisins
- 1 cup mixed dried fruit (cherries, apricots, dates, bananas)
- 1 cup peanuts
- Utensils: Mixing bowl, wooden spoon, resealable baggies

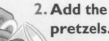

2. **Add the pretzels.**

3. **Add the peanuts.**

4. **Mix the ingredients together, breaking big pretzels into smaller bite-sized bits.**

5. **Serve your trail mix in a bowl as a party mix, or put it in plastic baggies to take on a hike.**

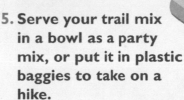

1. **Put the raisins and the dried fruit in a bowl. Break the clumps of fruit apart with your fingers.**

Turn the page for a recipe made with one of a horse's favorite foods: oats!

Cookie Dough's Oatmeal Cookies

See if you love these cookies as much as Cookie Dough does!

What You Need

- 🍪 3/4 cup vegetable oil
- 🍪 1 cup firmly packed brown sugar
- 🍪 1/2 cup sugar
- 🍪 1 egg
- 🍪 1/4 cup water
- 🍪 1 teaspoon vanilla
- 🍪 1/4 cup applesauce
- 🍪 3 cups oats
- 🍪 1 1/4 cup all-purpose flour
- 🍪 1 teaspoon salt
- 🍪 1/2 teaspoon baking soda
- 🍪 Utensils: Measuring cups and spoons, 2 large mixing bowls, cookie sheet, wooden spoon

Makes: 2 dozen berry soft cookies

1. **Ask a grown-up to preheat the oven to 350°F.**

2. **In one bowl, combine the vegetable oil, brown sugar, white sugar, egg, water, vanilla, and applesauce. Mix until creamy.**

3. In the other bowl, mix together the oats, flour, salt, and baking soda.

6. Bake your cookies in the oven for 12 to 15 minutes.

4. Add the dry ingredients to the wet ingredients a little at a time. Mix constantly, until smooth.

7. Ask an adult to remove the sheet from the oven. Let the cookies cool for 10 minutes before you remove them from the cookie sheet. Mmm, berry good!

5. Drop teaspoonfuls of batter onto a greased cookie sheet. Leave space between each clump of dough.

Turn the page for a special Ice Cream Island dessert!

Three Berries in a Banana Boat

Blueberry Muffin loves this treat, and so does her pony, Blueberry Sundae. Can you guess why?

1. **Wash all the berries—the raspberries, blueberries, and strawberries.**

What You Need

- 1 cup raspberries
- 1 cup blueberries
- 1 cup strawberries
- 1 ripe banana
- Vanilla ice cream
- Utensils: Measuring cups, ice cream scoop, serving dish, knife

2. **Remove the green tops from the strawberries.**

3. Put the berries in a dish and refrigerate overnight. This will make the berries taste yummier.

4. Remove the vanilla ice cream from the freezer and let it thaw a little.

5. Cut the banana in half (the long way). Keep the skin on, so the banana doesn't get squashed.

6. Peel the banana and lay it on a serving dish or in a bowl. Sprinkle some berries around the dish.

7. Add three scoops of ice cream. Sprinkle some more berries on top. Enjoy!

Turn the page for a yummy drink that Orange Blossom's pony loves!

Orange-y Orange Twist

Here's a fun drink that Orange Blossom's pony, Orange Twist, is here to make with you.

What You Need

- 2 cups milk
- 4 ounces of orange juice concentrate (1/2 of an 8 ounce can)
- 2 orange slices
- 1/4 teaspoon vanilla
- 2 cups of ice cubes
- Utensils: Blender, measuring cups and spoons, knife, glasses

  Makes: 2 servings

1. Place the ice cubes into the blender.

2. Scoop the orange juice concentrate into the blender.

3. **Now add the milk and vanilla.**

5. **Pour into glasses and add orange slices for decoration. To cut the orange, have an adult lay the fruit down on its side and slice through its center. Then slit a slice so that it attaches to the rim of your glass.**

Berry Funny

Q: Why couldn't the orange do her homework?

A: She couldn't concentrate!

4. **Blend for 2 minutes, until frothy.**

Honey Pie Pony's Answer Page

Honey Pie Pony's Spelling Bee Puzzle
(Page 20)

Honey Pie's Horse Sense
(Page 21)

Hidden Pie Pony and Friends Match-Up Game (Pages 22-23)

1. **Strawberry Shortcake's stripes are different.**
2. **One of Cookie Dough's ribbons fell off.**
3. **There are oranges in the tree instead of apples.**
4. **Ginger snap is holding a cookie jar.**
5. **Blueberry Sundae is smelling a flower.**
6. **Orange Blossom is waving.**
7. **A basket of oranges is under Orange Twist's hoof.**
8. **Orange Blossom has more pockets on her pants.**
9. **Angel Cake is wearing cowgirl boots.**
10. **Honey Pie is missing flowers on her tail.**

More Sweet
Strawberryland Adventures
COMING SOON!

To Our Berry Fun Friend,

Honey Pie Pony and I are berry glad you came to play! We hope you had fun on our filly friends adventure. You can continue to make projects of your berry own using your imagination and your Filly Craft Kit. Remember, in Strawberryland it's a whole lot of fun to make crafts, share sweet treats, and play great games together. Until our next adventure!

Your berry best friends,

Strawberry Shortcake

and **HONEY PIE**